KAMALA and MAYA'S BIG IDEA

By MEENA HARRIS

Illustrated by
ANA RAMÍREZ GONZÁLEZ

Balzer + Bray
An imprint of HarperCollins *Publishers*

"You know what should be out there?" Kamala
asked her sister, Maya.
"Us?" said Maya.
"A slide!" said Kamala.
"And a swing," Maya added.
"A playground!" they shouted together.

Kamala and Maya had an idea.
It was a very good idea. And a very big idea.
They were going to need help.

"Wouldn't it be great if there was a playground in the courtyard?" Maya said.

"That does sound nice," Mommy agreed.

"How can we make that happen?" Kamala asked.

"Well, I suppose the first step would be to ask the landlord—the person who owns the building."

So Kamala wrote a letter, and Maya drew a picture, and they went to see the landlord to discuss their idea.

The landlord thought about it
for less than a second.
"Hmmm. I don't think so, no."

That was not the answer they wanted.
But they weren't ready to give up.
That night, the sisters tried to think of
ways to turn a *no* into a *yes*.

They asked the other kids in the building
if they wanted a playground in the courtyard.
Did they? Of course they did—and they
had ideas too.

"Let's have a teeter-totter."

"And a basketball hoop."

"And flowers."

So Kamala wrote a longer letter, and
they went to see the landlord together.

DEAR LANDLORD,
RIGHT NOW THE COURTYARD OF
OUR BUILDING IS EMPTY AND NO
ONE USES IT.
IF THERE WERE SWINGS, KIDS
COULD FLY HIGH. ♥
IF THERE WAS A SANDBOX, KIDS
COULD BUILD.
IF THERE WAS A SLIDE, KIDS
COULD GO SO FAR, SO FAST.

CAN YOU BUILD IT, PLEASE?

The landlord thought about it for less than five seconds.

"A project this big is expensive. We don't have the money for that. Do your parents know you're here?"

This was not the answer they wanted.
But Kamala was not ready to give up.

"If we ask our parents and do it all ourselves, can we fix up the courtyard?"

The landlord thought about that for a whole *ten* seconds. Finally, he shrugged.

"If you can do it yourselves, sure."

This wasn't *exactly* the answer
they wanted. But it was a start.

The kids all spoke to their parents about their
ideas for the courtyard. They hung up posters
and knocked on neighbors' doors.

But they got the same answers from everyone.

"I'm sorry."
"Wow, that is a big job."
"Wish I could help."

Which they knew meant no, no, no.

But then Mr. Green stopped to talk.

"I work construction and I could maybe get some scrap lumber and some sand for a sandbox."

"Really?" Kamala said.

"Yes!" exclaimed Maya.

"Okay, I'll try."

It wasn't a yes. But right now *maybe* was the sweetest word they had ever heard. *Maybe* gave them hope.

The next weekend,
maybe turned into *yes*!

The kids all helped measure,
and Mr. Green cut the boards.

Then they sanded and
hammered and sanded some more.
Then came the actual sand.

They were all thanking Mr. Green when Ms. Lopez stopped to talk. "I work at a garage. Maybe they have an extra tire for a teeter-totter."

Another *maybe*!

In the weeks that followed, lots of *I don't knows* turned into *maybe*s and then *yes*es.

No one could do everything.
But everyone could do something.

Kamala and Maya wanted everyone to celebrate
the new playground so they made another big poster
inviting their neighbors to a potluck party.

There were hot dogs and hummus. Spicy chicken and potato salad. Strawberries and brownies and lemonade.

Mrs. Flores set up a sprinkler for the kids to run through.

Mr. Green brought the music.

Kamala admired the
new playground, but she
noticed there was still
one thing missing . . .

No one knew how to *make* a slide.

But Ms. Flores knew where they might *buy* one. "I teach at Emerson Elementary, and they are redoing their playground. Maybe we could buy the old slide?"

This was a different kind of maybe. A how-can-we-afford-that maybe. But now everyone was trying to find a way to turn that *maybe* into a *yes*.

"These brownies are delicious. Maybe we could have a bake sale?"

"We can all bring toys and books and have a sidewalk sale."

No one could do everything. But everyone could contribute something.

When the slide arrived at last, Maya and
Kamala got the first ride.

The landlord was impressed. "I want to shake your hands, girls," he said. "You did a good job. You *all* did a good job."

Kamala and Maya had an idea.
It was a very good idea. And a
very big idea.
And, with a lot of help, they made
it happen.

"Hooray for Kamala and Maya!"
"Hooray for the per-sisters!"
"What's next, Kamala?"
Kamala, looking up, said, "I'm wondering
what the view is like from the roof."

Growing up, I loved hearing stories about and seeing old pictures of my mom, Maya Harris, and aunt, Kamala Harris, as young girls in the 1970s. There's one picture in particular of my mom and aunt that I love: My mom is the one in the bandanna, my aunt in the bell-bottom jeans, and they're staring at the camera with fierce determination. They look like they've just conquered the world.

That's how I perceived them when I was younger. As I've gotten older, it's only become more true. They would go on to achieve great things, both as public interest lawyers dedicated to improving their communities. They always made sure I knew I could do anything, too.

A specific anecdote from their childhood always stuck with me: how they worked together to turn the unused courtyard in their apartment building into an area

for kids to play. It was an early lesson in the power of organizing and an example of what my grandmother, Shyamala Harris, a scientist and civil rights activist, always reminded us: each of us has a part to play, no matter how small.

By the time I had two daughters myself, I knew I had to write a book inspired by that story. This picture book is based on those events, but it incorporates fictional characters and details that draw on my own imaginative interpretation of what happened. I wanted to memorialize it not only for my girls but also for children across the world. I was so lucky to grow up with such strong female role models—my grandmother, my mother, and my aunt. I hope this book inspires a new generation of activists to know that they can be effective agents of change if they think creatively, engage their communities, and never, ever give up.

Balzer + Bray is an imprint of HarperCollins Publishers.

Kamala and Maya's Big Idea
Text copyright © 2020 by Meena Harris
Illustrations copyright © 2020 by Ana Ramírez González

ISBN 978-0-06-293740-7

The artist used mixed media (gouache and digital) to create the illustrations for this book.
Typography by Dana Fritts
20 21 22 23 24 PC 10 9 8 7 6 5 4
❖
First Edition